Billy Tibbles Moves Out!

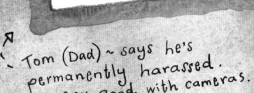

Valentina (that's Mom) →
Likes a peaceful house
and high-heeled
fluffy mules.
Total glamourpuss.

↑
Tom (Dad) ~ says he's
permanently harassed.
Not very good with cameras.

a
big purr
I thank you
to Sue
and
Sally

↑
Little Baby Eric.
Wise beyond his years.
Likes purple blankets.

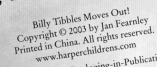

For Billy, Twinkle, and Little Eric

Billy Tibbles Moves Out!
Copyright © 2003 by Jan Fearnley
Printed in China. All rights reserved.
www.harperchildrens.com

Library of Congress Cataloging-in-Publication Data
Fearnley, Jan. Billy Tibbles moves out! / by Jan Fearnley. — 1st U.S. ed. p. cm.
Summary: When his little brother Eric moves into his room, Billy Tibbles the cat and his
family learn some of the good and bad things about sharing.
[1. Sharing—Fiction. 2. Family life—Fiction. 3. Cats—Fiction.]
ISBN 0-06-054650-6 I. Title PZ7.F2965Bi 2004 [E]—dc21 2002191325 CIP AC

1 2 3 4 5 6 7 8 9 10
❖
First Edition
First U.S. edition, HarperCollins Publishers, Inc., 2004
Originally published in Great Britain by HarperCollins Publishers Ltd., 2003

Twinkle - - - →
Trainee glamourpuss.
Likes glittery things
and teasing Billy.
(Secretly covets
the high-heeled
fluffy mules.)

Dad's foot

Billy's bottom

BillyTibbles
Moves Out!
by Jan Fearnley

Billy: being silly, as usual.
Likes skateboards and
teasing Twinkle.

HarperCollins*Publishers*

Billy Tibbles' bedroom was his favorite place.

Sometimes it was tidy.

Mostly it was messy.

Billy liked mess.

Billy's sister, Twinkle,
had her own room, too.
Billy wasn't allowed
in there . . .

but he didn't care.
He liked his room best.
It had his toys
and his books . . .

and his new
skateboard . . .

and his squeaky, creaky bed.
And best of all, Billy had it
all to himself.

But things changed when Mom said to Billy, "It's time Little Eric moved in."

Little Eric was the baby.

He slept in Mom and Dad's room, in Billy's old crib.

"He's big enough to share with you now," said Dad. "It'll be fun with you two boys together."

Billy thought about sharing his room with Little Eric.

And sharing his toys. Even sharing his new skateboard.

"It doesn't sound like fun to me!" said Billy. "I DON'T WANT TO!"

"Now then," said Dad.
"We ALL have to share in
this house—and that
means YOU, too, Billy!"

So the green crib was moved into Billy's room.
Billy didn't like it one bit.

"It's not fair!" he cried. "I don't want to share!"

"All big brothers have to share," said Mom, "and that means you, too, Billy."

So Little Eric moved in . . .

. . . and Billy Tibbles moved out!

"I'll show them!" he said. "I'm going to find somewhere better, somewhere all to myself."

Billy tried the bathroom. But the bathtub was hard
and uncomfortable, the faucet
went *drip, drip, drip, drip*—
and Twinkle kept
knocking on the door.

Billy tried the shed next.
But it was scary and
smelled like old boots.

And Billy *still* had to share . . . with the spiders!

"Ahh!" said Billy. "I'm not staying here!"

He raced back inside . . .

. . . just in time for a bedtime story.

But Twinkle wouldn't share, not even for a story.
She pushed and shoved. Billy wriggled and kicked.
Dad sent them both off to bed.

"I've told you before!" he said. "We all share in this
house, and that means you, Billy—
and you, too, Twinkle!"

It was dark on the stairs. Shadows lurked in every corner. For the first time, Billy was glad he wasn't by himself.

He held Twinkle's paw tightly.

As they padded down the hall, they heard a funny

noise coming from Billy's room.

Squeak . . . creak . . . *Boing!*

"Ooooh, Billy," whispered Twinkle. "I bet it's a

monster. A huge monster!"

"Don't be silly," Billy said. But he squeezed

Twinkle's paw even tighter, just in case.

Squeak . . . creak . . . *Boing!*

went the noise again.

"Let's see if it's a monster!" said Twinkle.

"You go first, Billy."

They tiptoed to the door and

peeked inside . . .

. . . and there *was* a little monster, (well, Little Eric) wide awake, and bouncing on Billy's bed!

"Hey!" yelled Billy. "Get off my bed, and that means you!"

"No!" said Little Eric. "Don't want to!"

Billy pounced—*Grrrr!*—and Billy bounced . . .

. . . very, very, very high.

Squeak . . . Little Eric flipped.

Creak . . . Twinkle joined in and did a somersault.

BOINNNG! Billy almost hit his head on the ceiling.

But he didn't mind. This kind of sharing was fun!

squeak!

creak!

boing!

Downstairs Mom and Dad had settled down to a nice, relaxing evening when . . .

"What is going on?" roared Dad. "Why aren't you asleep?"

"The bed's broken," said Twinkle.

"How did that happen?" asked Mom.

"We were sharing," said Billy. "Dad told us to."

"I'm bouncing!" said Little Eric.

Mom raised a weary paw. "No more explanations.

We'll figure things out in the morning. The boys can share with us tonight."

"Me too!" said Twinkle. "I like sharing."

Dad didn't look too happy. "Sharing? With all of you?" he groaned. "I don't want to!"

"Now then, Dad," said Billy. "Remember, everybody shares in this house— AND THAT MEANS YOU, *TOO*!

So MOVE OVER!"

And Dad moved over,
because dads have to share,
just like everyone else.

The children climbed onto
the big, cozy bed, and
eventually everybody
had a very good
night's sleep.

Well, almost everybody.